The Fifth String

The Fifth String

By

John Philip Sousa

The Illustrations by

Howard Chandler Christy

Published by Paganiniana Publications, Inc.
211 West Sylvania Avenue, Neptune City, N.J. 07753

Printed in Hong Kong

ISBN 0-87666-623-3

ACADEMY *of* MUSIC

DECEMBER 12TH — 8:00 P. M.

FIRST APPEARANCE IN AMERICA OF
THE RENOWNED TUSCAN
VIOLINIST

ANGELO
DIOTTI

ASSISTED BY

ARTISTS OF INTERNATIONAL
REPUTATION

DIRECTION OF MR. HENRY PERKINS

SECOND CONCERT OF SIGNOR DIOTTI
DECEMBER 14TH

The Fifth String

I

*T*HE coming of Diotti to America
had awakened more than usual interest in the man and his work. His
marvelous success as violinist in the
leading capitals of Europe, together with
many brilliant contributions to the lit-
erature of his instrument, had long been
favorably commented on by the critics
of the old world. Many stories of his
struggles and his triumphs had found
their way across the ocean and had been
read and re-read with interest.

Therefore, when Mr. Henry Perkins, the well-known impresario, announced with an air of conscious pride and pardonable enthusiasm that he had secured Diotti for a "limited" number of concerts, Perkins' friends assured that wide-awake gentleman that his foresight amounted to positive genius, and they predicted an unparalleled success for his star. On account of his wonderful ability as player, Diotti was a favorite at half the courts of Europe, and the astute Perkins enlarged upon this fact without regard for the feelings of the courts or the violinist.

On the night preceding Diotti's début in New York, he was the center of attraction at a reception given by Mrs. Llewellyn, a social leader, and a devoted patron of the arts. The violinist made a deep impression on those fortunate enough to be near him during the evening.   He won the respect of the men by his observations on matters of international interest, and the admiration of the gentler sex by his chivalric estimate of woman's influence in the world's progress, on which subject he talked with rarest good humor and delicately implied gallantry.

During one of those sudden and unexplainable lulls that always occur in general drawing-room conversations, Diotti turned to Mrs. Llewellyn and whispered : " Who is the charming young woman just entering ?"

" The beauty in white?"

" Yes, the beauty in white," softly echoing Mrs. Llewellyn's query. He leaned forward and with eager eyes gazed in admiration at the new-comer. He seemed hypnotized by the vision, which moved slowly from between the blue-tinted portières and stood for the

3

instant, a perfect embodiment of radiant womanhood, silhouetted against the silken drapery.

"That is Miss Wallace, Miss Mildred Wallace, only child of one of New York's prominent bankers."

"She is beautiful—a queen by divine right," cried he, and then with a mingling of impetuosity and importunity, entreated his hostess to present him.

And thus they met.

Mrs. Llewellyn's entertainments were celebrated, and justly so. At her receptions one always heard the best singers and players of the season, and Epicurus' soul could rest in peace, for her chef had an international reputation. Oh, remember, you music-fed ascetic, many, aye, very many, regard the transition from Tschaikowsky to terrapin, from Beethoven to burgundy with hearts aflame with anticipatory joy—and Mrs. Llewellyn's dining-room was crowded.

Miss Wallace and Diotti had wandered into the conservatory.

"A desire for happiness is our common heritage," he was saying in his richly melodious voice.

"But to define what constitutes happiness is very difficult," she replied.

"Not necessarily," he went on; "if the motive is clearly within our grasp, the attainment is possible."

"For example?" she asked.

"The miser is happy when he hoards his gold; the philanthropist when he distributes his. The attainment is identical, but the motives are antipodal."

"Then one possessing sufficient motives could be happy without end?" she suggested doubtingly.

"That is my theory. The Niobe of old had happiness within her power."

"The gods thought not," said she; "in their very pity they changed her into stone, and with streaming eyes she ever tells the story of her sorrow."

"But are her children weeping?" he asked. "I think not. Happiness can bloom from the seeds of deepest woe," and in a tone almost reverential, he continued: "I remember a picture in one of our Italian galleries that always impressed me as the ideal image of maternal happiness. It is a painting of the Christ-mother standing by the body of the Crucified. Beauty was still hers, and the dress of grayish hue, nun-like in its simplicity, seemed more than royal robe. Her face, illumined as with a light from heaven, seemed inspired with this thought: 'They have killed Him—they have killed my son! Oh, God, I thank Thee that His suffering is at an end!' And as I gazed at the holy face, another light seemed to change it by degrees from saddened motherhood to triumphant woman! Then came: 'He is not dead, He but sleeps; He will rise again, for He is the best beloved of the Father!'"

"Still, fate can rob us of our patrimony," she replied, after a pause.

"Not while life is here and eternity beyond," he said, reassuringly.

"What if a soul lies dormant and will not arouse?" she asked.

"There are souls that have no motive low enough for earth, but only high enough for heaven," he said, with evident intention, looking almost directly at her.

"Then one must come who speaks in nature's tongue," she continued.

"And the soul will then awake," he added earnestly.

7

"But is there such a one?" she asked.

"Perhaps," he almost whispered, his thought father to the wish.

"I am afraid not," she sighed. "I studied drawing, worked diligently and, I hope, intelligently, and yet I was quickly convinced that a counterfeit presentment of nature was puny and insignificant. I painted Niagara. My friends praised my effort. I saw Niagara again—I destroyed the picture."

"But you must be prepared to accept the limitations of man and his work," said the philosophical violinist.

"Annihilation of one's own identity in the moment is possible in nature's domain—never in man's. The resistless, never-ending rush of the waters, madly churning, pitilessly dashing against the rocks below; the mighty roar of the loosened giant; that was

8

"*But you must be prepared to accept the limitations of man and his work.*"

Niagara. My picture seemed but a smear of paint."

" Still, man has won the admiration of man by his achievements," he said.

"Alas, for me," she sighed, " I have not felt it."

" Surely you have been stirred by the wonders man has accomplished in music's realm?" Diotti ventured.

" I never have been." She spoke sadly and reflectively.

" But does not the passion-laden theme of a master, or the marvelous feeling of a player awaken your emotions?" persisted he.

She stood leaning lightly against a pillar by the fountain. " I never hear a pianist, however great and famous, but I see the little cream-colored hammers within the piano bobbing up and down like acrobatic brownies. I never hear the plaudits of the crowd for the

artist and watch him return to bow his
thanks, but I mentally demand that
these little acrobats, each resting on an
individual pedestal, and weary from his
efforts, shall appear to receive a share
of the applause.

"When I listen to a great singer,"
continued this world-defying skeptic,
"trilling like a thrush, scampering over
the scales, I see a clumsy lot of ah, ah,
ahs, awkwardly, uncertainly ambling up
the gamut, saying, 'were it not for us
she could not sing thus—give us our
meed of praise.'"

Slowly he replied: "Masters have
written in wondrous language and masters have played with wondrous power."

"And I so long to hear," she said,
almost plaintively. "I marvel at the
invention of the composer and the skill
of the player, but there I cease."

He looked at her intently. She was

standing before him, not a block of chiseled ice, but a beautiful, breathing woman. He offered her his arm and together they made their way to the drawing-room.

"Perhaps, some day, one will come who can sing a song of perfect love in perfect tones, and your soul will be attuned to his melody."

"Perhaps—and good-night," she softly said, leaving his arm and joining her friends, who accompanied her to the carriage.

II

THE intangible something that places the stamp of popular approval on one musical enterprise, while another equally artistic and as cleverly managed languishes in a condition of unendorsed greatness, remains one of the unsolved mysteries.

When a worker in the vineyard of music or the drama offers his choicest tokay to the public, that fickle coquette may turn to the more ordinary and less succulent concord. And the worker and the public itself know not why.

It is true, Diotti's fame had preceded him, but fame has preceded others and has not always been proof against financial disaster. All this preliminary,—and it is but necessary to recall that on the evening of December the twelfth Diotti made his initial bow in New York, to an audience that completely filled every available space in the Academy of Music—a representative audience, distinguished alike for beauty, wealth and discernment.

When the violinist appeared for his solo, he quietly acknowledged the cordial reception of the audience, and immediately proceeded with the business of the evening. At a slight nod from him the conductor rapped attention, then launched the orchestra into the introduction of the concerto, Diotti's favorite, selected for the first number. As the violinist turned to the conductor he faced slightly to the left and in a direct line with the second proscenium box. His poise was admirable. He was handsome, with the olive-tinted warmth of his southern home—fairly tall, straight-limbed and lithe—a picture of poetic grace. His was the face of a man who trusted without reserve, the manner of one who believed implicitly, feeling that good was universal and evil accidental.

As the music grew louder and the orchestra approached the peroration of the preface of the coming solo, the violinist raised his head slowly. Suddenly his eyes met the gaze of the solitary occupant of the second proscenium box. His face flushed. He looked inquiringly, almost appealingly, at her. She sat immovable and serene, a lace-framed vision in white.

It was she who, since he had met her, only the night before, held his very soul in thraldom.

Suddenly his eyes met the gaze of the solitary occupant. She sat immovable and serene.

He lifted his bow, tenderly placing it on the strings. Faintly came the first measures of the theme. The melody, noble, limpid and beautiful, floated in dreamy sway over the vast auditorium, and seemed to cast a mystic glamour over the player. As the final note of the first movement was dying away, the audience, awakening from its delicious trance, broke forth into spontaneous bravos.

Mildred Wallace, scrutinizing the program, merely drew her wrap closer about her shoulders and sat more erect. At the end of the concerto the applause was generous enough to satisfy the most exacting *virtuoso*. Diotti unquestionably had scored the greatest triumph of his career. But the lady in the box had remained silent and unaffected throughout.

The poor fellow had seen only her dur-

ing the time he played, and the mighty
cheers that came from floor and galleries struck upon his ear like the echoes
of mocking demons. Leaving the stage
he hurried to his dressing-room and
sank into a chair. He had persuaded
himself she should not be insensible to
his genius, but the dying ashes of his
hopes, his dreams, were smouldering,
and in his despair came the thought:
"I am not great enough for her. I am
but a man; her consort should be a god.
Her soul, untouched by human passion
or human skill, demands the power of
god-like genius to arouse it."

Music lovers crowded into his dressing-room, enthusiastic in their praises.
Cards conveying delicate compliments
written in delicate chirography poured
in upon him, but in vain he looked for
some sign, some word from her.

Quickly he left the theater and sought his hotel.

A menacing cloud obscured the wintry moon. A clock sounded the midnight hour.

He threw himself upon the bed and almost sobbed his thoughts, and their burden was:

"I am not great enough for her. I am but a man. I am but a man!"

III

PERKINS called in the morning. Perkins was happy—Perkins was positively joyous, and Perkins was self-satisfied. The violinist had made a great hit. But Perkins, confiding in the white-coated dispenser who concocted his *matin Martini*, very dry, an hour before, said he regarded the success due as much to the management as to the artist. And Perkins believed it. Perkins usually took all the credit for a success, and with charming consistency placed all responsibility for failure on the shoulders of the hapless artist.

When Perkins entered Diotti's room

he found the violinist heavy-eyed and dejected. "My dear Signor," he began, showing a large envelope bulging with newspaper clippings, "I have brought the notices. They are quite the limit, I assure you. Nothing like them ever heard before—all tuned in the same key, as you musical fellows would say," and Perkins cocked his eye.

Perkins enjoyed a glorious reputation with himself for bright sayings, which he always accompanied with a cock of the eye. The musician not showing any visible appreciation of the manager's metaphor, Perkins immediately proceeded to uncock his eye.

"Passed the box-office coming up," continued this voluble enlightener; "nothing left but a few seats in the top gallery. We'll stand them on their heads to-morrow night—see if we don't." Then he handed the bursting

envelope of notices to Diotti, who list-
lessly put them on the table at his side.

"Too tired to read, eh?" said Perkins, and then with the advance-agent
instinct strong within him he selected a
clipping, and touching the violinist on
the shoulder: "Let me read this one to
you. It is by Herr Totenkellar. He
is a hard nut to crack, but he did himself proud this time. Great critic when
he wants to be."

Perkins cleared his throat and began:
"Diotti combines tremendous feeling
with equally tremendous technique.
The entire audience was under the
witchery of his art." Diotti slowly neg-
atived that statement with bowed head.
"His tone is full, round and clear; his
interpretation lends a story-telling charm
to the music ; for, while we drank deep
at the fountain of exquisite melody, we
saw sparkling within the waters the

lights of Paradise. New York never has heard his equal. He stands alone, pre-eminent, an artistic giant."

"Now, that's what I call great," said the impresario, dramatically; "when you hit Totenkellar that way you are good for all kinds of money."

Perkins took his hat and cane and moved toward the door. The violinist arose and extended his hand wearily. "Good-day" came simultaneously; then "I'm off. We'll turn 'em away to-morrow; see if we don't!" Whereupon Perkins left Diotti alone in his misery.

IV

IT was the evening of the fourteenth. In front of the Academy a strong-lunged and insistent tribe of gentry, known as ticket speculators, were reaping a rich harvest. They represented a beacon light of hope to many tardy patrons of the evening's entertainment, especially to the man who had forgotten his wife's injunction "to be sure to buy the tickets on the way down town, dear, and get them in the family circle, not too far back." This man's intentions were sincere, but his newspaper was unusually interesting that morning. He was deeply engrossed in an

article on the causes leading to matri-
monial infelicities when his 'bus passed
the Academy box-office.

He was six blocks farther down town
when he finished the article, only to
find that it was a carefully worded
advertisement for a new patent medi-
cine, and of course he had not time to
return. "Oh, well," said he, " I'll get
them when I go up town to-night."

But he did not. So with fear in his
heart and a red-faced woman on his
arm he approached the box-office.
" Not a seat left," sounded to his hen-
pecked ears like the concluding words
of the black-robed judge: "and may the
Lord have mercy upon your soul." But
a reprieve came, for one of the aforesaid
beacon lights of hope rushed forward,
saying: " I have two good seats, not
far back, and only ten apiece." And
the gentleman with fear in his heart

and the red-faced woman on his arm passed in.

They saw the largest crowd in the history of the Academy. Every seat was occupied, every foot of standing room taken. Chairs were placed in the side aisles. The programs announced that it was the second appearance in America of Angelo Diotti, the renowed Tuscan violinist.

The orchestra had perfunctorily ground out the overture to " Der Frei-schuetz," the baritone had stentorianly emitted " Dio Possente," the soprano was working her way through the closing measures of the mad scene from " Lu-cia," and Diotti was number four on the program. The conductor stood beside his platform, ready to ascend as Diotti appeared.

The audience, ever ready to act when those on the stage cease that occupation, gave a splendid imitation of the historic last scene at the Tower of Babel. Having accomplished this to its evident satisfaction, the audience proceeded, like the closing phrase of the "Goetterdaemmerung" Dead March, to become exceedingly quiet—then expectant.

This expectancy lasted fully three minutes. Then there were some impatient handclappings. A few persons whispered: "Why is he late?" "Why doesn't he come?" "I wonder where Diotti is," and then came unmistakable signs of impatience. At its height Perkins appeared, hesitatingly. Nervous and jerky he walked to the center of the stage, and raised his hand begging silence. The audience was stilled.

"Ladies and gentlemen," he falteringly said, "Signor Diotti left his hotel at seven o'clock and was driven to the Academy. The call-boy rapped at his

dressing-room, and not receiving a reply, opened the door to find the room
empty. We have despatched searchers
in every direction and have sent out a
police alarm. We fear some accident
has befallen the Signor. We ask your
indulgence for the keen disappointment,
and beg to say that your money will be
refunded at the box-office."

Diotti had disappeared as completely as though the earth had swallowed
him.

V

MY DEAREST SISTER: You
doubtless were exceedingly mystified and troubled over the report that
was flashed to Europe regarding my
sudden disappearance on the eve of my
second concert in New York.

Fearing, sweet Francesca, that you
might mourn me as dead, I sent the
cablegram you received some weeks
since, telling you to be of good heart
and await my letter. To make my action thoroughly understood I must give
you a record of what happened to me
from the first day I arrived in America. I found a great interest mani-

fested in my première, and socially everything was done to make me happy.

Mrs. James Llewellyn, whom, you no doubt remember, we met in Florence the winter of 18—, immediately after I reached New York arranged a reception for me, which was elegant in the extreme. But from that night dates my misery.

You ask her name?—Mildred Wallace. Tell me what she is like, I hear you say. Of graceful height, willowy and exquisitely molded, not over twenty-four, with the face of a Madonna; wondrous eyes of darkest blue, hair indescribable in its maze of tawny color —in a word, the perfection of womanhood. In half an hour I was her abject slave, and proud in my serfdom. When I returned to the hotel that evening I could not sleep. Her image ever was before me, elusive and shadowy.

And yet we seemed to grow farther and farther apart—she nearer heaven, I nearer earth.

The next evening I gave my first and what I fear may prove my last concert in America. The vision of my dreams was there, radiant in rarest beauty. Singularly enough, she was in the direct line of my vision while I played. I saw only her, played but for her, and cast my soul at her feet. She sat indifferent and silent. "Cold?" you say. No! No! Francesca, not cold; superior to my poor efforts. I realized my limitations. I questioned my genius. When I returned to bow my acknowledgments for the most generous applause I have ever received, there was no sign on her part that I had interested her, either through my talent or by appeal to her curiosity. I hoped against hope that some word might come from her, but I was doomed to disappointment. The critics were fulsome in their praise and the public was lavish with its plaudits, but I was abjectly miserable. Another sleepless night and I was determined to see her. She received me most graciously, although I fear she thought my visit one of vanity—wounded vanity— and me petulant because of her lack of appreciation.

Oh, sister mine, I knew better. I knew my heart craved one word, however matter-of-fact, that would rekindle the hope that was dying within me.

Hesitatingly, and like a clumsy yokel, I blurted: "I have been wondering whether you cared for the performance I gave?"

"It certainly ought to make little difference to you," she replied; "the public was enthusiastic enough in its endorsement."

"But I want your opinion," I pleaded.

"My opinion would not at all affect the almost unanimous verdict," she replied calmly.

"And," I urged desperately, "you were not affected in the least?"

Very coldly she answered, "Not in the least;" and then fearlessly, like a princess in the Palace of Truth: "If ever a man comes who can awaken my heart, frankly and honestly I will confess it."

"Perhaps such a one lives," I said, "but has yet to reach the height to win you—your—"

"Speak it," she said, "to win my love!"

"Yes," I cried, startled at her candor, "to win your love." Hope slowly rekindled within my breast, and then

31

with half-closed eyes, and wooingly, she said :

"No drooping Clytie could be more constant than I to him who strikes the chord that is responsive in my soul."

Her emotion must have surprised her, but immediately she regained her placidity and reverted no more to the subject.

I went out into the gathering gloom. Her words haunted me. A strange feeling came over me. A voice within me cried : "Do not play to-night. Study! study! Perhaps in the full fruition of your genius your music, like the warm western wind to the harp, may bring life to her soul."

I fled, and I am here. I am delving deeper and deeper into the mysteries of my art, and I pray God each hour that He may place within my grasp the wondrous music His blessed angels

sing, for the soul of her I love is at-
tuned to the harmonies of heaven.
Your affectionate brother,
ANGELO.
ISLAND OF BAHAMA, January 2.

VI

*W*HEN Diotti left New York so precipitately he took passage on a coast line steamer sailing for the Bahama Islands. Once there, he leased a small *cay*, one of a group off the main land, and lived alone and unattended, save for the weekly visits of an old fisherman and his son, who brought supplies of provisions from the town miles away. His dwelling-place, surrounded with palmetto trees, was little more than a rough shelter. Diotti arose at daylight, and after a simple repast, betook himself to practise. Hour after hour he would let his muse run riot with his fingers. Lovingly he wooed the strings with plaintive song, then conquering and triumphant would be his theme. But neither satisfied him. The vague dream of a melody more beautiful than ever man had heard dwelt hauntingly on. the borders of his imagination, but was no nearer realization than when he began. As the day's work closed, he wearily placed the violin within its case, murmuring, " Not yet, not yet; I have not found it."

Days passed, weeks crept slowly on; still he worked, but always with the same result. One day, feverish and excited, he played on in monotone almost listless. His tired, over-wrought brain denied a further thought. His arm and fingers refused response to his will. With an uncontrollable outburst of grief and anger he dashed the violin to the floor, where it

35

lay a hopeless wreck. Extending his arms he cried, in the agony of despair: " It is of no use! If the God of heaven will not aid me, I ask the prince of darkness to come."

A tall, rather spare, but well-made and handsome man appeared at the door of the hut. His manner was that of one evidently conversant with the usages of good society.

" I beg pardon," said the musician, surprised and visibly nettled at the intrusion, and then with forced politeness he asked: " To whom am I indebted for this unexpected visit? "

"Allow me," said the stranger taking a card from his case and handing it to the musician, who read: " Satan," and, in the lower left-hand corner, " Prince of Darkness."

" I am the Prince," said the stranger, bowing low.

There was no hint of the pavement-made ruler in the information he gave, but rather of the desire of one gentleman to set another right at the beginning. The musician assumed a position of open-mouthed wonder, gazing steadily at the visitor.

"Satan?" he whispered hoarsely.

"You need help and advice," said the visitor, his voice sounding like that of a disciple of the healing art, and implying that he had thoroughly diagnosed the case.

"No, no," cried the shuddering violinist; "go away. I do not need you."

"I regret I can not accept that statement as gospel truth," said Satan, sarcastically, "for if ever a man needed help, you are that man."

"But not from you," replied Diotti.

"That statement is discredited also

by your outburst of a few moments ago when you called upon me.''

" I do not need you,'' reiterated the musician. " I will have none of you!" and he waved his arm toward the door, as if he desired the interview to end.

"I came at your behest, actuated entirely by kindness of heart,'' said Satan.

Diotti laughed derisively, and Satan, showing just the slightest feeling at Diotti's behavior, said reprovingly: "If you will listen a moment, and not be so rude to an utter stranger, we may reach some conclusion to your benefit.''

" Get thee behind—''

" I know exactly what you were about to say. Have no fears on that score. I have no demands to make and no impossible compacts to insist upon.''

"I have heard of you before,'' knowingly spoke the violinist, nodding his head sadly.

"No doubt you have," smilingly. "My reputation, which has suffered at the hands of irresponsible people, is not of the best, and places me at times in awkward positions. But I am beginning to live it down." The stranger looked contrition itself. "To prove my sincerity I desire to help you win her love," emphasizing her.

"How can you help me?"

"Very easily. You have been wasting time, energy and health in a wild desire to play better. The trouble lies not with you."

"Not with me?" interrupted the violinist, now thoroughly interested.

"The trouble lies not with you," repeated the visitor, "but with the miserable violin you have been using and have just destroyed," and he pointed to the shattered instrument.

Tears welled from the poor violinist's eyes as he gazed on the fragments of his beloved violin, the pieces lying scattered about as the result of his unfortunate anger.

"It was a Stradivarius," said Diotti, sadly.

"Had it been a Stradivarius, an Amati or a Guarnerius, or a host of others rolled into one, you would not have found in it the melody to win the heart of the woman you love. Get a better and more suitable instrument."

"Where is one?" earnestly interrogated Diotti, vaguely realizing that Satan knew.

"In my possession," Satan replied.

"She would hate me if she knew I had recourse to the powers of darkness to gain her love," bitterly interposed Diotti.

Satan, wincing at this uncomplimentary allusion to himself, replied rather warmly: "My dear sir, were it not for the fact that I feel in particularly good spirits this morning, I should resent your ill-timed remarks and leave you to end your miserable existence with rope or pistol," and Satan pantomimed both suicidal contingencies.

"Do you want the violin or not?"

"I might look at it," said Diotti, resolving mentally that he could go so far without harm.

"Very well," said Satan. He gave a long whistle.

An old man, bearing a violin case, came within the room. He bowed to the wondering Diotti, and proceeded to open the case. Taking the instrument out the old man fondled it with loving and tender solicitude, pointing out its many beauties—the exquisite blending of the curves, the evenness of the grain, the peculiar coloring, the lovely contour of the neck, the graceful outlines of the body, the scroll, rivaling the creations of the ancient sculptors, the solidity of the bridge and its elegantly carved heart, and, waxing exceedingly enthusiastic, holding up the instrument and looking at it as one does at a cluster of gems, he added, "the adjustment of the strings."

"That will do," interrupted Satan, taking the violin from the little man, who bowed low and ceremoniously took his departure. Then the devil, pointing to the instrument, asked: "Isn't it a beauty?"

The musician, eying it keenly, replied: "Yes, it is, but not the kind of violin I play on."

*Taking the instrument out the old man fondled it with lov-
ing and tender solicitude.*

"Oh, I see," carelessly observed the other, " you refer to that extra string."

" Yes," answered the puzzled violinist, examining it closely.

"Allow me to explain the peculiar characteristics of this magnificent instrument," said his satanic majesty. "This string," pointing to the G, " is the string of pity; this one," referring to the third, " is the string of hope; this," plunking the A, "is attuned to love, while this one, the E string, gives forth sounds of joy.

" You will observe," went on the visitor, noting the intense interest displayed by the violinist, " that the position of the strings is the same as on any other violin, and therefore will require no additional study on your part."

" But that extra string?" interrupted Diotti, designating the middle one on the violin, a vague foreboding rising within him.

"That," said Mephistopheles, solemnly, and with no pretense of sophistry, "is the string of death, and he who plays upon it dies at once."

"The—string—of—death!" repeated the violinist almost inaudibly.

"Yes, the string of death," Satan repeated, "and he who plays upon it dies at once. But," he added cheerfully, "that need not worry you. I noticed a marvelous facility in your arm work. Your staccato and spiccato are wonderful. Every form of bowing appears child's play to you. It will be easy for you to avoid touching the string."

"Why avoid it? Can it not be cut off?"

"Ah, that's the rub. If you examine the violin closely you will find that the string of death is made up of the extra lengths of the other four strings. To cut it off would destroy the others, and then pity, hope, love and joy would cease to exist in the soul of the violin."

"How like life itself," Diotti reflected, "pity, hope, love, joy end in death, and through death they are born again."

"That's the idea, precisely," said Satan, evidently relieved by Diotti's logic and quick perception.

The violinist examined the instrument with the practised eye of an expert, and turning to Satan said: "The four strings are beautifully white and transparent, but this one is black and odd looking.

"What is it wrapped with?" eagerly inquired Diotti, examining the death string with microscopic care.

"The fifth string was added after an

45

unfortunate episode in the Garden of Eden, in which I was somewhat concerned," said Satan, soberly. "It is wrapped with strands of hair from the first mother of man." Impressively then he offered the violin to Diotti.

"I dare not take it," said the perplexed musician; "it's from—"

"Yes, it is directly from there, but I brought it from heaven when I—I left," said the fallen angel, with remorse in his voice. "It was my constant companion there. But no one in my domain—not I, myself—can play upon it now, for it will respond neither to our longing for pity, hope, love, joy, nor even death," and sadly and retrospectively Satan gazed into vacancy; then, after a long pause: "Try the instrument!"

Diotti placed the violin in position

and drew the bow across the string of
joy, improvising on it. Almost instantly
the birds of the forest darted hither and
thither, caroling forth in gladsome
strains. The devil alone was sad, and
with emotion said :

"It is many, many years since I
have heard that string."

Next the artist changed to the string
of pity, and thoughts of the world's
sorrows came over him like a pall.

" Wonderful, most wonderful!" said
the mystified violinist; "with this instrument I can conquer the world!"

" Aye, more to you than the world,"
said the tempter, "a woman's love."

A woman's love—to the despairing
suitor there was one and only one in this
wide, wide world, and her words, burning their way into his heart, had made
this temptation possible: "No droop-

47

ing Clytie could be more constant than I to him who strikes the chord that is responsive in my soul."

Holding the violin aloft, he cried exultingly: "Henceforth thou art mine, though death and oblivion lurk ever near thee!"

VII

PERKINS, seated in his office, threw the morning paper aside. "It's no use," he said, turning to the office boy, "I don't believe they ever will find him, dead or alive. Whoever put up the job on Diotti was a past grand master at that sort of thing. The silent assassin that lurks in the shadow of the midnight moon is an explosion of dynamite compared to the party that made way with Diotti. You ask, why should they kill him? My boy, you don't know the world. They were jealous of his enormous hit, of our dazzling success. Jealousy did it."

49

The "they" of Perkins comprised rival managers, rival artists, newspaper critics and everybody at large who would not concede that the attractions managed by Perkins were the "greatest on earth."

"We'll never see his like again— come in!" this last in answer to a knock.

Diotti appeared at the open door. Perkins jumped like one shot from a catapult, and rushing toward the silent figure in the doorway exclaimed: "Bless my soul, are you a ghost?"

"A substantial one," said Diotti with a smile.

"Are you really here?" continued the astonished impresario, using Diotti's arm as a pump handle and pinching him at the same time.

When they were seated Perkins plied Diotti with all manner of questions: "How did it happen?" "How did you escape?'' and the like, all of which Diotti parried with monosyllabic replies, finally saying: '' I was dissatisfied with my playing and went away to study.''

'' Do you know that the failure to fulfill your contract has cost me at least ten thousand dollars?'' said the shrewd manager, the commercial side of his nature asserting itself.

''All of which I will pay,'' quietly replied the artist. ''Besides I am ready to play now, and you can announce a concert within a week if you like.''

'' If I like?'' cried the hustling Perkins. '' Here, James,'' calling his office boy, '' run down to the printer's and give him this,'' making a note of the various sizes of ''paper'' he desired, '' and tell Mr. Tompkins that Diotti is back and will give a concert next Tuesday. Tell Smith to prepare the newspaper 'ads' and notices immediately.''

In an hour Perkins had the entire machinery of his office in motion. Within twenty-four hours New York had several versions of the disappearance and return, all leading to one common point—that Diotti would give a concert the coming Tuesday evening.

The announcement of the reappearance of the Tuscan contained a line to the effect that the violinist would play for the first time his new suite—a meditation on the emotions.

He had not seen Mildred.

As he came upon the stage that night the lights were turned low, and naught but the shadowy outlines of player and violin were seen. His reception by the audience was not enthusiastic. They evidently remembered the disappointment caused by his unexpected disappearance, but this unfriendly attitude soon gave way to evidences of kindlier feelings.

Mildred was there, more beautiful than ever, and to gain her love Diotti would have bartered his soul that moment.

The first movement of the suite was entitled " Pity," and the music flowed like melodious tears. A subdued sob rose and fell with the sadness of the theme.

Mildred's eyes were moistened as she fixed them on the lone figure of the player.

Now the theme of pity changed to hope, and hearts grew brighter under the spell. The next movement depicted joy. As the *virtuoso's* fingers darted here and there, his music seemed the very laughter of fairy voices, the earth looked roses and sunshine, and Mildred, relaxing her

53

position and leaning forward in the box, with lips slightly parted, was the picture of eager happiness.

The final movement came. Its subject was love. The introduction depicted the Arcadian beauty of the trysting place, love-lit eyes sought each other intuitively and a great peace brooded over the hearts of all. Then followed the song of the Passionate Pilgrim:

"If music and sweet poetry agree,
As they must needs, the sister and the brother,
Then must the love be great 'twixt thee and
me
Because thou lov'st the one, and I the other.

    *   *   *   *   *   *

Thou lov'st to hear the sweet melodious sound
That Phœbus' lute (the queen of music) makes;
And I in deep delight, am chiefly drown'd
When as himself to singing he betakes.

One god is god of both, as poets feign,
One knight loves both, and both in thee re-
    main."

Grander and grander the melody rose, voicing love's triumph with wondrous sweetness and palpitating rhythm. Mildred, her face flushed with excitement, a heavenly fire in her eyes and in an attitude of supplication, reveled in the glory of a new found emotion.

As the violinist concluded his performance an oppressive silence pervaded the house, then the audience, wild with excitement, burst into thunders of applause. In his dressing-room Diotti was besieged by hosts of people, congratulating him in extravagant terms.

Mildred Wallace came, extending her hands. He took them almost reverently. She looked into his eyes, and he knew he had struck the chord responsive in her soul.

VIII

*T*HE sun was high in the heavens when the violinist awoke. A great weight had been lifted from his heart; he had passed from darkness into dawn. A messenger brought him this note:

My Dear Signor Diotti—I am at home this afternoon, and shall be delighted to see you and return my thanks for the exquisite pleasure you gave me last evening. Music, such as yours, is indeed the voice of heaven. Sincerely,
                              Mildred Wallace.

The messenger returned with this reply:

My Dear Miss Wallace—I will call at three to-day. *Gratefully,*
                              Angelo Diotti.

56

She looked into his eyes, and he knew he had struck the chord responsive in her soul.

He watched the hour drag from eleven to twelve, then counted the minutes to one, and from that time until he left the hotel each second was tabulated in his mind. Arriving at her residence, he was ushered into the drawing-room. It was fragrant with the perfume of violets, and he stood gazing at her portrait expectant of her coming.

Dressed in simple white, entrancing in her youthful freshness, she entered, her face glowing with happiness, her eyes languorous and expressive. She hastened to him, offering both hands. He held them in a loving, tender grasp, and for a moment neither spoke. Then she, gazing clearly and fearlessly into his eyes, said: " My heart has found its melody! "

He, kneeling like Sir Gareth of old: " The song and the singer are yours forever."

She, bidding him arise : "And I forever yours." And wondering at her
boldness, she added, "I know and feel
that you love me—your eyes confirmed
your love before you spoke." Then,
convincingly and ingenuously, "I knew
you loved me the moment we first met.
Then I did not understand what that
meant to you, now I do."

He drew her gently to him, and the
motive of their happiness was defined
in sweet confessions: "My love, my
life—My life, my love."

The magic of his music had changed
her very being, the breath of love was
in her soul, the vision of love was dancing in her eyes. The child of marble,
like the statue of old, had come to life:

> "*And not long since*
> *I was a cold, dull stone! I recollect*
> *That by some means I knew that I was stone;*
> *That was the first dull gleam of consciousness;*

I became conscious of a chilly self,
A cold, immovable identity.
I knew that I was stone, and knew no more!
Then, by an imperceptible advance,
Came the dim evidence of outer things,
Seen—darkly and imperfectly—yet seen
The walls surrounding me, and I, alone.
That pedestal—that curtain—then a voice
That called on Galatea! At that word,
Which seemed to shake my marble to the core,
That which was dim before, came evident.
Sounds, that had hummed around me, indis-
tinct,
Vague, meaningless—seemed to resolve them-
selves
Into a language I could understand;
I felt my frame pervaded by a glow
That seemed to thaw my marble into flesh;
Its cold, hard substance throbbed with active
life,
My limbs grew supple, and I moved—I lived!
Lived in the ecstasy of a new-born life!
Lived in the love of him that fashioned me!
Lived in a thousand tangled thoughts of hope."

Day after day he came ; they told their

love, their hopes, their ambitions. She assumed absolute proprietorship in him. She gloried in her possession.

He was born into the world, nurtured in infancy, trained in childhood and matured into manhood, for one express purpose—to be hers alone. Her ownership ranged from absolute despotism to humble slavery, and he was happy through it all.

One day she said: "Angelo, is it your purpose to follow your profession always?"

"Necessarily, it is my livelihood," he replied.

"But do you not think that after we stand at the altar, we never should be separated?"

"We will be together always," said he, holding her face between his palms, and looking with tender expression into her inquiring eyes.

"But I notice that women cluster around you after your concerts—and shake your hand longer than they should—and talk to you longer than they should—and go away looking self-satisfied!" she replied brokenly, much as a little girl tells of the theft of her doll.

"Nonsense," he said, smiling, "that is all part of my profession; it is not me they care for, it is the music I give that makes them happy. If, in my playing, I achieve results out of the common, they admire me!" and he kissed away the unwelcome tears.

"I know," she continued, "but lately, since we have loved each other, I can not bear to see a woman near you. In my dreams again and again an indefinable shadow mockingly comes and cries to me, 'he is not to be yours, he is to be mine.'"

Diotti flushed and drew her to him. "Darling," his voice carrying conviction, "I am yours, you are mine, all in all, in life here and beyond!" And as she sat dreaming after he had gone, she murmured petulantly, "I wish there were no other women in the world."

Her father was expected from Europe on the succeeding day's steamer. Mr. Wallace was a busy man. The various gigantic enterprises he served as president or director occupied most of his time. He had been absent in Europe for several months, and Mildred was anxiously awaiting his return to tell him of her love.

When Mr. Wallace came to his residence the next morning, his daughter met him with a fond display of filial affection; they walked into the drawing-room, hand in hand; he saw a picture of the violinist on the piano. "Who's the handsome young fellow?" he asked, looking at the portrait with the satisfaction a man feels when he sees a splendid type of his own sex.

"That is Angelo Diotti, the famous violinist," she said, but she could not add another word.

As they strolled through the rooms he noticed no less than three likenesses of the Tuscan. And as they passed her room he saw still another on the *chiffonnier*.

"Seems to me the house is running wild with photographs of that fiddler," he said.

For the first time in her life she was self-conscious: "I will wait for a more opportune time to tell him," she thought.

In the scheme of Diotti's appearance in New York there were to be two more concerts. One was to be given that evening. Mildred coaxed her father to accompany her to hear the violinist. Mr. Wallace was not fond of music; "it had been knocked out of him on the farm up in Vermont, when he was a boy," he would apologetically explain, and besides he had the old puritanical abhorrence of stage people — putting them all in one class—as puppets who danced or played or talked for an idle and unthinking public.

So it was with the thought of a wasted evening that he accompanied Mildred to the concert.

The entertainment was a repetition of the others Diotti had given, and at its end, Mildred said to her father : "Come, I want to congratulate Signor Diotti in person."

"That is entirely unnecessary," he replied.

"It is my desire," and the girl led

64

the unwilling parent back of the scenes and into Diotti's dressing-room.

Mildred introduced Diotti to her father, who after a few commonplaces lapsed into silence. The daughter's enthusiastic interest in Diotti's performance and her tender solicitude for his weariness after the efforts of the evening, quickly attracted the attention of Mr. Wallace and irritated him exceedingly.

When father and daughter were seated in their carriage and were hurriedly driving home, he said: "Mildred, I prefer that you have as little to say to that man as possible."

"What do you object to in him?" she asked.

"Everything. Of what use is a man who dawdles away his time on a fiddle; of what benefit is he to mankind ? Do fiddlers build cities? Do they delve into the earth for precious metals? Do they sow the seed and harvest the grain? No, no; they are drones—the barnacles of society."

"Father, how can you advance such an argument? Music's votaries offer no apologies for their art. The husband-man places the grain within the breast of Mother Earth for man's material welfare; God places music in the heart of man for his spiritual development. In man's spring time, his bridal day, music means joy. In man's winter time, his burial day, music means comfort. The heaven-born muse has added to the happiness of the world. Diotti is a great genius. His art brings rest and tranquillity to the wearied and despairing," and she did not speak again until they had reached the house.

The lights were turned low when father and daughter went into the drawing-room. Mr. Wallace felt that he had failed to convince Mildred of the utter worthlessness of fiddlers, big or little, and as one dissatisfied with the outcome of a contest, re-entered the lists.

"He has visited you?"

"Yes, father."

"Often?"

"Yes, father," spoken calmly.

"Often?" louder and more imperiously repeated the father, as if there must be some mistake.

"Quite often," and she sat down, knowing the catechizing would be likely to continue for some minutes.

"How many times, do you think?"

She rose, walked into the hallway; took the card basket from the table, returned and seated herself beside her father, emptying its contents into her lap. She picked up a card. It read

67

"Angelo Diotti," and she called the name aloud. She took up another and again her lips voiced the beloved name. "Angelo Diotti," she continued, repeating at intervals for a minute. Then looking at her father : " He has called thirty-two times ; there are thirty-one cards here and on one occasion he forgot his card-case."

"Thirty-two!" said the father, rising angrily and pacing the floor.

" Yes, thirty-two. I remember all of them distinctly."

Her father came over to her, half coaxingly, half seriously. " Mildred, I wish his visits to cease; people will imagine there is a romantic attachment between you."

" There is, father," out it came, "he loves me and I love him."

" What !" shouted Mr. Wallace, and

"I love him with my whole soul. There is none other in the world for him, nor for me."

then severely, " this must cease immediately."

She rose quietly and led her father
over to the mantel. Placing a hand on
each of his shoulders she said :

" Father, I will obey you implicitly
if you can name a reasonable objection
to the man I love. But you can not.
I love him with my whole soul. I love
him for the nobility of his character,
and because there is none other in the
world for him, nor for me."

IX

*O*LD *SANDERS* as boy and man
had been in the employ of the
banking and brokerage firm of Wallace
Brothers for two generations. The firm
gradually had advanced his position until now he was confidential adviser and
general manager, besides having an interest in the profits of the business.

He enjoyed the friendship of Mr.
Wallace, and had been a constant visitor at his house from the first days of
that gentleman's married life. He himself was alone in the world, a confirmed
bachelor. He had seen Mildred creep
from babyhood into childhood, and bud

from girlhood to womanhood. To Mildred he was one of that numerous army of brevet relations known as "granpop," "pop," or "uncle." To her he was Uncle Sanders.

If the old man had one touch of human nature in him it was a solicitude for Mildred's future—an authority arrogated to himself—to see that she married the right man; but even that was directed to her material gain in this world's goods, and not to any sentimental consideration for her happiness. He flattered himself that by timely suggestion he had "stumped" at least half a dozen would-be candidates for Mildred's hand. He pooh-poohed love as a necessity for marital felicity, and would enforce his argument by quoting from the bard:

"All lovers swear more performance than they are able, and yet reserve an ability that they never perform; vowing more than the perfection of ten, and discharging less than the tenth part of one."

"You can get at a man's income," he would say, "but not at his heart. Love without money won't travel as far as money without love," and many married people whose bills were overdue wondered if the old fellow was not right.

He was cold-blooded and generally disliked by the men under him. The more evil-minded gossips in the bank said he was in league with "Old Nick." That, of course, was absurd, for it does not necessarily follow, because a man suggests a means looking to an end, disreputable though it be, that he has Mephistopheles for a silent partner. The conservative element among the employees would not openly venture so far, but rather thought if his satanic majesty and old Sanders ran a race, the former would come in a bad second, if he were not distanced altogether.

The old man always reached the office at nine. Mr. Wallace usually arrived a half hour later, seldom earlier, which was so well understood by Sanders that he was greatly surprised when he walked into the president's office, the morning after that gentleman had attended Diotti's concert, to find the head of the firm already there and apparently waiting for him.

"Sanders," said the banker, "I want your advice on a matter of great importance and concern to me."

Sanders came across the room and stood beside the desk.

"Briefly as possible, I am much exercised about my daughter."

The old man moved up a chair and buried himself in it. Pressing his elbows tightly against his sides, he drew his neck in, and with the tips of his right hand fingers consorted and coquetted with their like on the opposite hand; then he simply asked, "Who is the man?"

"He is the violinist who has created such a sensation here, Angelo Diotti."

"Yes, I've seen the name in print," returned the old man.

"He has bewitched Mildred. I never have seen her show the least interest in a man before. She never has appeared to me as an impressionable girl or one that could easily be won."

"That is very true," ejaculated Sanders; "she always seemed tractable and open to reason in all questions of love and courting. I can recall several instances where I have set her right by my estimation of men, and invariably she has accepted my views."

"And mine until now," said the father, and then he recounted his experience of the night before. "I had hoped she would not fall in love, but be a prop and comfort to me now that I am alone. I am dismayed at the prospect before me."

Then the old man mused: "In the chrysalis state of girlhood, a parent arranges all the details of his daughter's future; when and whom she shall marry. 'I shall not allow her to fall in love until she is twenty-three,' says the fond parent. 'I shall not allow her to marry until she is twenty-six,' says the fond parent. 'The man she marries will be the one I approve of, and then she will live happy ever after,' concludes the fond parent."

Deluded parent! false prophet! The

anarchist, Love, steps in and disdains all laws, rules and regulations. When finally the father confronts the defying daughter, she calmly says, "Well, what are you going to do about it?" And then tears, forgiveness, complete capitulation, and, sometimes, she and her husband live happily ever afterwards.

"We must find some means to end this attachment. A union between a musician and my daughter would be most mortifying to me. Some plan must be devised to separate them, but she must not know of it, for she is impatient of restraint and will not brook opposition."

"Are you confident she really loves this violinist?"

"She confessed as much to me," said the perturbed banker.

Old Sanders tapped with both hands

on his shining cranium and asked, "Are you confident he loves her?"

"No. Even if he does not, he no doubt makes the pretense, and she believes him. A man who fiddles for money is not likely to ignore an opportunity to angle for the same commodity," and the banker, with a look of scorn on his face, threw himself back into the chair.

" Does she know that you do not approve of this man?"

"I told her that I desired the musician's visits to cease."

"And her answer?"

"She said she would obey me if I could name one reasonable objection to the man, and then, with an air of absolute confidence in the impossibility of such a contingency, added, ' But you can not.' "

"Yes, but you must," said Sanders. "Mildred is strangely constituted. If she loves this man, her love can be more deadly to the choice of her heart than her hate to one she abhors. The impatience of restraint you speak of and her very inability to brook opposition can be turned to good account now." And old Sanders again tapped in the rhythm of a dirge on his parchment-bound cranium.

"Your plan?" eagerly asked the father, whose confidence in his secretary was absolute.

"I would like to study them together. Your position will be stronger with Mildred if you show no open opposition to the man or his aspirations; bring us together at your house some evening, and if I can not enter a wedge of discontent, then they are not as others."

* * * * * *

Mildred was delighted when her father told her on his return in the

78

evening that he was anxious to meet
Signor Diotti, and suggested a dinner
party within a few days. He said he
would invite Mr. Sanders, as that gentleman, no doubt, would consider it a
great privilege to meet the famous musician. Mildred immediately sent an
invitation to Diotti, adding a request
that he bring his violin and play for
Uncle Sanders, as the latter had found
it impossible to attend his concerts during the season, yet was fond of music,
especially violin music.

X

THE little dinner party passed off pleasantly, and as old Sanders lighted his cigar he confided to Diotti, with a braggart's assurance, that when he was a youngster he was the best fiddler for twenty miles around. "I tell you there is nothing like a fiddler to catch a petticoat," he said, with a sharp nudge of his elbow into Diotti's ribs. "When I played the Devil's Dream there wasn't a girl in the country could keep from dancing, and 'Rosalie, the Prairie Flower,' brought them on their knees to me every time;" then after a pause, "I don't believe people fiddle as well nowadays as they did in the good old times," and he actually sighed in remembrance.

Mildred smiled and whispered to Diotti. He took his violin from the case and began playing. It seemed to her as if from above showers of silvery merriment were falling to earth. The old man watched intently, and as the player changed from joy to pity, from love back to happiness, Sanders never withdrew his gaze. His bead-like eyes followed the artist; he saw each individual finger rise and fall, and the bow bound over the finger-board, always avoiding, never coming in contact with the middle string. Suddenly the old man beat a tattoo on his cranium and closed his eyes, apparently deep in thought.

As Diotti ceased playing, Sanders applauded vociferously, and moving toward the violinist, said: "Magnificent!

I never have heard better playing! What is the make of your violin?"

Diotti, startled at this question, hurriedly put the instrument in its case; "Oh, it is a famous make," he drawled.

"Will you let me examine it?" said the elder, placing his hand on the case.

"I never allow any one to touch my violin," replied Diotti, closing the cover quickly.

"Why; is there a magic charm about it, that you fear other hands may discover?" queried the old man.

"I prefer that no one handle it," said the *virtuoso* commandingly.

"Very well," sighed the old man resignedly, "there are violins and violins, and no doubt yours comes within that category," this half sneeringly.

"Uncle," interposed Mildred tactfully, "you must not be so persistent. Signor Diotti prizes his violin highly and will not allow any one to play upon it but himself,'' and the look of relief on Diotti's face amply repaid her.

Mr. Wallace came in at that moment, and with perfunctory interest in his guest, invited him to examine the splendid collection of revolutionary relics in his study.

'' I value them highly,'' said the banker, '' both for patriotic and ancestral reasons. The Wallaces fought and died for their country, and helped to make this land what it is.''

The father and the violinist went to the study, leaving the daughter and old Sanders in the drawing-room. The old man, seating himself in a large armchair, said: '' Mildred, my dear, I do not wonder at the enormous success of this Diotti.''

'' He is a wonderful artist,'' replied Mildred; ''critics and public alike place him among the greatest of his profession."

" He is a good-looking young fellow, too," said the old man.

" I think he is the handsomest man I ever have seen," replied the girl.

" Where does he come from? " continued Sanders.

" St. Casciano, a small town in Tuscany."

" Has he a family? "

" Only a sister, whom he loves dearly," good-naturedly answered the girl.

" And no one else? " continued the seemingly garrulous old man.

" None that I have heard him speak of. No, certainly not," rather impetuously replied Mildred.

" How old is he? " continued the old man.

"Twenty-eight next month; why do you wish to know?" she quizzically asked.

"Simply idle curiosity," old Sanders carelessly replied. "I wonder if he is in love with any one in Tuscany?"

"Of course not; how could he be?" quickly rejoined the girl.

"And why not?" added old Sanders.

"Why? Because, because—he is in love with some one in America."

"Ah, with you, I see," said the old man, as if it were the greatest discovery of his life; "are you sure he has not some beautiful sweetheart in Tuscany as well as here?"

"What a foolish question," she replied. "Men like Angelo Diotti do not fall in love as soldiers fall in line. Love to a man of his nobility is too serious to be treated so lightly."

"Very true, and that's what has excited my curiosity!" whereupon the old man smoked away in silence.

"Excited your curiosity!" said Mildred. "What do you mean?"

"It may be something; it may be nothing; but my speculative instinct has been aroused by a strange peculiarity in his playing."

"His playing is wonderful!" replied Mildred proudly.

"Aye, more than wonderful! I watched him intently," said the old man; "I noted with what marvelous facility he went from one string to the other. But however rapid, however difficult the composition, he steadily avoided one string; in fact, that string remained untouched during the entire hour he played for us."

"Perhaps the composition did not

call for its use," suggested Mildred, unconscious of any other meaning in the old man's observation, save praise for her lover.

"Perhaps so, but the oddity impressed me; it was a new string to me. I have never seen one like it on a violin before."

"That can scarcely be, for I do not remember of Signor Diotti telling me there was anything unusual about his violin."

"I am sure it has a fifth string."

"And I am equally sure the string can be of no importance or Angelo would have told me of it," Mildred quickly rejoined.

"I recall a strange story of Paganini," continued the old man, apparently not noticing her interruption; "he became infatuated with a lady of high rank, who was insensible of the admiration he had for her beauty.

"He composed a love scene for two strings, the 'E' and 'G,' the first was to personate the lady, the second himself. It commenced with a species of dialogue, intending to represent her indifference and his passion; now sportive, now sad; laughter on her part and tears from him, ending in an apotheosis of loving reconciliation. It affected the lady to that degree that ever after she loved the violinist."

"And no doubt they were happy?" Mildred suggested smilingly.

"Yes," said the old man, with assumed sentiment, "even when his profession called him far away, for she had made him promise her he never would play upon the two strings whose music had won her heart, so those strings were mute, except for her."

The old man puffed away in silence for a moment, then with logical directness continued : "Perhaps the string that's mute upon Diotti's violin is mute for some such reason."

"Nonsense," said the girl, half impatiently.

"The string is black and glossy as the tresses that fall in tangled skeins on the shoulders of the dreamy beauties of Tuscany. It may be an idle fancy, but if that string is not a woven strand from some woman's crowning glory, then I have no discernment."

"You are jesting, uncle," she replied, but her heart was heavy already.

"Ask him to play on that string; I'll wager he'll refuse," said the old man, contemptuously.

"He will not refuse when I ask him, but I will not to-night," answered the unhappy girl, with forced determination. Then, taking the old man's hands, she said: "Good-night, I am going to my room; please make my excuses to Signor Diotti and father," and wearily she ascended the stairs.

Mr. Wallace and the violinist soon after joined old Sanders, fresh cigars were lighted and regrets most earnestly expressed by the violinist for Mildred's "sick headache."

"No need to worry; she will be all right in the morning," said Sanders, and he and the violinist buttoned their coats tightly about them, for the night was bitter cold, and together they left the house.

In her bed-chamber Mildred stood looking at the portrait of her lover. She studied his face long and intently, then crossing the room she mechanically took a volume from the shelf, and as she opened it her eyes fell on these lines:

" How art thou fallen from Heaven, O Lucifer, son of the Morning ! "

   *   *   *   *   *   *

Old Sanders builded better than he knew.

X I

*W*HEN Diotti and old Sanders left
the house they walked rapidly
down Fifth Avenue. It was after eleven,
and the streets were bare of pedestrians,
but blinking-eyed cabs came up the avenue, looking at a distance like a trail
of Megatheriums, gliding through the
darkness. The piercing wind made the
men hasten their steps, the old man by
a semi-rotary motion keeping up with
the longer strides and measured tread of
the younger.

When they reached Fourteenth Street,
the elder said, " I live but a block from
here," pointing eastward; " what do

you say to a hot toddy? It will warm
the cockles of your heart; come over to
my house and I'll mix you the best
drink in New York."

The younger thought the suggestion
a good one and they turned toward the
house of old Sanders.

It was a neat, red brick, two-story
house, well in from the street, off the
line of the more pretentious buildings on
either side. As the old man opened the
iron gate, the police officer on the beat
passed; he peered into the faces of the
men, and recognizing Sanders, said,
"tough night, sir."

"Very," replied the addressed.

"All good old gentlemen should be in
bed at this hour," said the officer, lift-
ing one foot after the other in an effort
to keep warm, and in so doing showing
little terpsichorean grace.

"It's only the shank of the evening,

officer," rejoined the old man, as he fumbled with the latch key and finally opened the door. The two men entered and the officer passed on.

Every man' has a fad. One will tell you he sees nothing in billiards or pool or golf or tennis, but will grow enthusiastic over the scientific possibilities of mumble-peg ; you agree with him, only you substitute "skittles" for "mumble-peg."

Old Sanders' fad was mixing toddies and punches.

"The nectar of the gods pales into nothingness when compared with a toddy such as I make," said he. "Ambrosia may have been all right for the degenerates of the old Grecian and Roman days, but an American gentleman demands a toddy—a hot toddy." And then he proceeded with circumspection and dignity to demonstrate the process of decocting that mysterious beverage.

The two men took off their overcoats and went into the sitting-room. A pile of logs burned brightly in the fire-place. The old man threw another on the burning heap, filled the kettle with water and hung it over the fire. Next he went to the sideboard and brought forth the various ingredients for the toddy.

"How do you like America?" said the elder, with commonplace indifference, as he crunched a lump of sugar in the bottom of the glass, dissolving the particles with a few drops of water.

"Very much, indeed," said the Tuscan, with the air of a man who had answered the question before.

"Great country for girls!" said Sanders, pouring a liberal quantity of Old Tom gin in the glass and placing it where it gradually would get warm.

"And for men!" responded Diotti, enthusiastically.

"Men don't amount to much here, women run everything," retorted the elder, while he repeated the process of preparing the sugar and gin in the second glass. The kettle began to sing.

"That's music for you," chuckled the old man, raising the lid to see if the water had boiled sufficiently. "Do you know I think a dinner horn and a singing kettle beat a symphony all hollow for real down-right melody," and he lifted the kettle from the fire-place.

Diotti smiled.

With mathematical accuracy the old man filled the two tumblers with boiling water.

"Try that," handing a glass of the toddy to Diotti; "you will find it all right," and the old man drew an armchair toward the fire-place, smacking his lips in anticipation.

The violinist placed his chair closer to the fire and sipped the drink.

" Your country is noted for its beautiful women?"

" We have exquisite types of femininity in Tuscany," said the young man, with patriotic ardor.

"Any as fine looking as—as—as— well, say the young lady we dined with to-night?"

" Miss Wallace?" queried the Tuscan.

" Yes, Miss Wallace," this rather impatiently.

" She is very beautiful," said Diotti, with solemn admiration.

" Have you ever seen any one prettier?" questioned the old man, after a second prolonged sip.

"I have no desire to see any one more beautiful," said the violinist, feeling that the other was trying to draw him out, and determined not to yield.

"You will pardon the inquisitiveness of an old man, but are not you musicians a most impressionable lot?"

"We are human," answered the violinist.

"I imagined you were like sailors and had a sweetheart in every port."

"That would be a delightful prospect to one having polygamous aspirations, but for myself, one sweetheart is enough," laughingly said the musician.

"Only one! Well, here's to her! With this nectar fit for the gods and goddesses of Olympus, let us drink to her," said old Sanders, with convivial dignity, his glass raised on high. "Here's wishing health and happiness to the dreamy-eyed Tuscan beauty, whom you love and who loves you."

"Stop!" said Diotti; "we will drink to the first part of that toast," and holding his glass against that of his bibulous host, continued: "To the dreamy-eyed women of my country, exacting of their lovers; obedient to their parents and loyal to their husbands," and his voice rose in sonorous rhythm with the words.

"Now for the rest of the toast, to the one you love and who loves you," came from Sanders.

"To the one I love and who loves me, God bless her!" fervently cried the guest.

"Is she a Tuscan?" asked old Sanders slyly.

"She is an angel!" impetuously answered the violinist.

" Then she is an American!" said the old man gallantly.

"She is an American," repeated Diotti, forgetting himself for the instant.

" Let me see if I can guess her name," said old Sanders. " It's—it's Mildred Wallace!" and his manner suggested a child solving a riddle.

The violinist, about to speak, checked himself and remained silent.

" I sincerely pity Mildred if ever she falls in love," abstractedly continued the host while filling another glass.

" Pray why?" was anxiously asked.

The old man shifted his position and assumed a confidential tone and attitude: "Signor Diotti, jealousy is a more universal passion than love itself. Environment may develop our character, influence our tastes and even soften our features, but heredity determines the intensity of the two leading passions, love and jealousy. Mildred's mother was a beautiful woman, but consumed with an overpowering jealousy of her husband. It was because she loved him. The body-guard of jealousy—envy, malice and hatred—were not in her composition. When Mildred was a child of twelve I have seen her mother suffer the keenest anguish because Mr. Wallace fondled the child. She thought the child had robbed her of her husband's love."

"Such a woman as Miss Wallace would command the entire love and admiration of her husband at all times," said the artist.

"If she should marry a man she simply likes, her chances for happiness would be normal."

"In what manner?" asked the lover.

"Because she would be little concerned about him or his actions."

"Then you believe," said the musician, "that the man who loves her and
whom she loves should give her up because her chances of happiness would be
greater away from him than with him?"

"That would be an unselfish love,"
said the elder.

"Suppose they have declared their
passion?" asked Diotti.

"A parting before doubt and jealousy
had entered her mind would let the image of her sacrificing lover live within
her soul as a tender and lasting memory;
he always would be her ideal," and the
accent old Sanders placed on *always* left
no doubt of his belief.

"Why should doubt and jealousy enter her life?" said the violinist, falling
into the personal character of the discus-
sion despite himself.

"My dear sir, from what I observed
to-night, she loves you. You are a dan-

gerous man for a jealous woman to love. You are not a cloistered monk, you are a man before the public; you win the admiration of many; some women do not hesitate to show you their preference. To a woman like Mildred that would be torture; she could not and would not separate the professional artist from the lover or husband.''

And Diotti, remembering Mildred's words, could not refute the old man's statements.

'' If you had known her mother as I did,'' continued the old man, realizing his argument was making an impression on the violinist, ''you would see the agony in store for the daughter if she married a man such as you, a public servant, a public favorite.''

'' I would live my life not to excite her suspicions or jealousy,'' said the artist, with boyish enthusiasm and simplicity.

"Foolish fellow," retorted Sanders, skeptically; "women imagine, they don't reason. A scented note unopened on the dressing table can cause more unhappiness to your wife than the loss ot his country to a king. My advice to you is: do not marry; but if you must, choose one who is more interested in your gastronomic felicity than in your marital constancy."

Diotti was silent. He was pondering the words of his host. Instead of seeing in Mildred a possibly jealous woman, causing mental misery, she appeared a vision of single-hearted devotion. He felt: "To be loved by such a one is bliss beyond the dreams of this world."

XII

A *TIPSY* man is never interesting,
and Sanders in that condition
was no exception. The old man arose
with some effort, walked toward the
window and, shading his eyes, looked
out. The snow was drifting, swept
hither and thither by the cutting wind
that came through the streets in great
gusts. Turning to the violinist, he said,
" It's an awful night; better remain here
until morning. You'll not find a cab; in
fact, I will not let you go while this
storm continues," and the old man
raised the window, thrusting his head
out for an instant. As he did so the icy

blast that came in settled any doubt in the young man's mind and he concluded to stop over night.

It was nearly two o'clock; Sanders showed him to his room and then returned down stairs to see that everything was snug and secure. After changing his heavy shoes for a pair of old slippers and wrapping a dressing gown around him, the old man stretched his legs toward the fire and sipped his toddy.

"He isn't a bad sort for a violinist," mused the old man; "if he were worth a million, I believe I'd advise Wallace to let him marry her. A fiddler! A million! Sounds funny," and he laughed shrilly.

He turned his head and his eyes caught sight of Diotti's violin case resting on the center table. He staggered from the chair and went toward it; opening the lid softly, he lifted the silken coverlet placed over the instrument and examined the strings intently. "I am right," he said; "it is wrapped with hair, and no doubt from a woman's head. Eureka!" and the old man, happy in the discovery that his surmises were correct, returned to his chair and his toddy.

He sat looking into the fire. The violin had brought back memories of the past and its dead. He mumbled, as if to the fire, "she loved me; she loved my violin. I was a devil; my violin was a devil," and the shadows on the wall swayed like accusing spirits. He buried his face in his hands and cried piteously, "I was so young; too young to know." He spoke as if he would conciliate the ghastly shades that moved restlessly up and down, when suddenly —"Sanders, don't be a fool!"

He ambled toward the table again.

"I wonder who made the violin? He would not tell me when I asked him to-night; thank you for your pains, but I will find out myself," and he took the violin from the case. Holding it with the light slanting over it, he peered inside, but found no inscription. "No maker's name—strange," he said. He tiptoed to the foot of the stairs and listened intently; "he must be asleep; he won't hear me," and noiselessly he closed the door. "I guess if I play a tune on it he won't know."

He took the bow from its place in the case and tightened it. He listened again. "He is fast asleep," he whispered. "I'll play the song I always played for her—until," and the old man repeated the words of the refrain:

"Fair as a lily, joyous and free,
Light of the prairie home was she;

Every one who knew her felt the gentle power
Of Rosalie, the Prairie Flower."

He sat again in the arm-chair and placed the violin under his chin. Tremulously he drew the bow across the middle string, his bloodless fingers moving slowly up and down.

The theme he played was the melody to the verse he had just repeated, but the expression was remorse.

*   *   *   *   *   *

Diotti sat upright in bed. " I am positive I heard a violin!" he said, holding one hand toward his head in an attitude of listening. He was wide awake. The drifting snow beat against the window panes and the wind without shrieked like a thousand demons of the night. He could sleep no more. He arose and hastily dressed. The room was bitterly cold; he was shivering. He thought of the crackling logs in the fire-place below. He groped his way along the darkened staircase. As he opened the door leading into the sitting-room the fitful gleam of the dying embers cast a ghastly light over the face of a corpse.

Diotti stood a moment, his eyes transfixed with horror. The violin and bow still in the hands of the dead man told him plainer than words what had happened. He went toward the chair, took the instrument from old Sanders' hands and laid it on the table. Then he knelt beside the body, and placing his ear close over the heart, listened for some sign of life, but the old man was beyond human aid.

He wheeled the chair to the side of the room and moved the body to the sofa. Gently he covered it with a robe. The awfulness of the situation forced itself upon him, and bitterly he blamed

himself. The terrible power of the instrument dawned upon him in all its
force. Often he had played on the strings
telling of pity, hope, love and joy, but
now, for the first time, he realized what
that fifth string meant.

"I must give it back to its owner."

"If you do you can never regain it,"
whispered a voice within.

"I do not need it," said the violinist,
almost audibly.

"Perhaps not," said the voice, "but
if her love should wane how would you
rekindle it? Without the violin you
would be helpless."

"Is it not possible that, in this old
man's death, all its fatal power has been
expended?"

He went to the table and took the instrument from its place. "You won her
for me; you have brought happiness
and sunshine into my life. No! No!

I can not, will not give you up," then placing the violin and bow in its case he locked it.

The day was breaking. In an hour the baker's boy came. Diotti went to the door, gave him a note addressed to Mr. Wallace and asked him to deliver it at once. The boy consented and drove rapidly away.

Within an hour Mr. Wallace arrived; Diotti told the story of the night. After the undertaker had taken charge of the body he found on the dead man's neck, just to the left of the chin, a dullish, black bruise which might have been caused by the pressing of some blunt instrument, or by a man's thumb. Considering it of much importance, he notified the coroner, who ordered an inquest.

At six o'clock that evening a jury was impaneled, and two hours later its verdict was reported.

XIII

*O**N** leaving the house of the dead man Diotti walked wearily to his hotel. In flaring type at every street corner he saw the announcement for Thursday evening, March thirty-first, of Angelo Diotti's last appearance : " To-night I play for the last time," he murmured in a voice filled with deepest regret.

The feeling of exultation so common to artists who finally reach the goal of their ambition was wanting in Diotti this morning. He could not rid himself of the memory of Sanders' tragic death. The figure of the old man clutching the violin and staring with glassy eyes into the dying fire would not away.

When he reached the hotel he tried to rest, but his excited brain banished every thought of slumber. Restlessly he moved about the room, and finally dressing, he left the hotel for his daily call on Mildred. It was after five o'clock when he arrived. She received him coldly and without any mark of affection.

She had heard of Mr. Sanders' death; her father had sent word. "It shocked me greatly," she said; "but perhaps the old man is happier in a world far from strife and care. When we realize all the misery there is in this world we often wonder why we should care to live." Her tone was despondent, her face was drawn and blanched, and her eyes gave evidence of weeping.

Diotti divined that something beyond

sympathy for old Sanders' sudden death racked her soul. He went toward her and lovingly taking her hands, bent low and pressed his lips to them; they were cold as marble.

"Darling," he said; "something has made you unhappy. What is it?"

"Tell me, Angelo, and truly; is your violin like other violins?"

This unexpected question came so suddenly he could not control his agitation.

"Why do you ask?" he said.

"You must answer me directly!"

"No, Mildred; my violin is different from any other I have ever seen," this hesitatingly and with great effort at composure.

"In what way is it different?" she almost demanded.

"It is peculiarly constructed; it has an extra string. But why this sudden

interest in the violin? Let us talk of
you, of me, of both, of our future," said
he with enforced cheerfulness.

"No, we will talk of the violin. Of
what use is the extra string?"

"None whatever," was the quick reply.

"Then why not cut it off?"

"No, no, Mildred; you do not understand," he cried; "I can not do
that."

"You can not do it when I ask it?"
she exclaimed.

"Oh Mildred, do not ask me; I can
not, can not do it," and the face of the
affrighted musician told plainer than
words of the turmoil raging in his soul.

"You made me believe that I was the
only one you loved," passionately she
cried; "the only one; that your happiness
was incomplete without me. You led
me into the region of light only to make

the darkness greater when I descended to earth again. I ask you to do a simple thing and you refuse; you refuse because another has commanded you."

"Mildred, Mildred; if you love me do not speak thus!"

And she, with imagination greater than reasoning power, at once saw a Tuscan beauty and Diotti mutually pledging their love with their lives.

"Go," she said, pointing to the door, "go to the one who owns you, body and soul; then say that a foolish woman threw her heart at your feet and that you scorned it!" She sank to the sofa.

He went toward the door, and in a voice that sounded like the echo of despair, protested: "Mildred, I love you; love you a thousand times more than I do my life. If I should destroy the string, as you ask, love and hope would leave me forevermore. Death would

not be robbed of its terror!" and with
bowed head he went forth into the twi-
light.

She ran to the window and watched
his retreating figure as he vanished.
"Uncle Sanders was right; he loves another woman, and that string binds them
together. He belongs to her!" Long
and silently she stood by the window,
gazing at the shadowing curtain of the
coming night. At last her face softened.
"Perhaps he does not love her now, but
fears her vengeance. No, no; he is not
a coward! I should have approached
him differently; he is proud, and may-
be he resented my imperative manner,"
and a thousand reasons why he should
or should not have removed that string
flashed through her mind.

"I will go early to the concert to-
night and see him before he plays.
Uncle Sanders said he did not touch that

string when he played. Of course he
will play on it for me, even if he will not
cut it off, and then if he says he loves
me, and only me, I will believe him. , I
want to believe him; I want to believe
him," all this in a semi-hysterical way
addressed to the violinist's portrait on
the piano.

When she entered her carriage an hour
later, telling the coachman to drive direct
to the stage-door of the Academy, she
appeared more fascinating than ever before.

She was sitting in his dressing-room
waiting for him when he arrived. He
had aged years in a day. His step was
uncertain, his eyes were sunken and his
hand trembled. His face brightened as
she arose, and Mildred met him in the
center of the room. He lifted her hand
and pressed a kiss upon it.

"Angelo, dear," she said in repentant

tone; "I am sorry I pained you this afternoon; but I am jealous, so jealous of you."

"Jealous?" he said smilingly; "there is no need of jealousy in our lives; we love each other truly and only."

"That is just what I think, we will never doubt each other again, will we?"

"Never!" he said solemnly.

He had placed his violin case on the table in the room. She went to it and tapped the top playfully; then suddenly said: "I am going to look at your violin, Angelo," and before he could interfere, she had taken the silken coverlet off and was examining the instrument closely. "Sure enough, it has five strings; the middle one stands higher than the rest and is of glossy blackness. Uncle Sanders was right; it is a woman's hair!

"Why is that string made of hair?" she asked, controlling her emotion.

"Only a fancy," he said, feigning indifference.

"Though you would not remove it at my wish this afternoon, Angelo; I know you will not refuse to play on it for me now."

He raised his hands in supplication. "Mildred! Mildred! Stop! do not ask it!"

"You refuse after I have come repentant, and confessing my doubts and fears? Uncle Sanders said you would not play upon it for me; he told me it was wrapped with a woman's hair, the hair of the woman you love."

"I swear to you, Mildred, that I love but you!"

"Love me? Bah! And another woman's tresses sacred to you? Another woman's pledge sacred to you? I asked you to remove the string; you refused. I ask you now to play upon it; you refuse," and she paced the room like a caged tigress.

"I will watch to-night when you play," she flashed. "If you do not use that string we part forever."

He stood before her and attempted to take her hand; she repulsed him savagely.

Sadly then he asked: "And if I do play upon it?"

"I am yours forever—yours through life—through eternity," she cried passionately.

The call-boy announced Diotti's turn; the violinist led Mildred to a seat at the entrance of the stage. His appearance was the signal for prolonged and enthusiastic greeting from the enormous audience present. He clearly was the idol of the metropolis.

The lights were lowered, a single calcium playing with its soft and silvery

"*I will watch to-night when you play. If you do not use that string we part forever.*"

rays upon his face and shoulders. The expectant audience scarcely breathed as he began his theme. It was pity—pity molded into a concord of beautiful sounds, and when he began the second movement it was but a continuation of the first; his fingers sought but one string, that of pity. Again he played, and once more pity stole from the violin.

When he left the stage Mildred rushed to him. "You did not touch that string; you refuse my wish?" and the sounds of mighty applause without drowned his pleading voice.

"I told you if you refused me I was lost to you forever! Do you understand?"

Diotti returned slowly to the center of the stage and remained motionless until the audience subsided. Facing Mildred, whose color was heightened by the intensity of her emotion, he began softly to play. His fingers sought the string of Death. The audience listened with breathless interest. The composition was weirdly and strangely fascinating.

The player told with wondrous power of despair,—of hope, of faith; sunshine crept into the hearts of all as he pictured the promise of an eternal day; higher and higher, softer and softer grew the theme until it echoed as if it were afar in the realms of light and floating o'er the waves of a golden sea.

Suddenly the audience was startled by the snapping of a string; the violin and bow dropped from the nerveless hands of the player. He fell helpless to the stage.

Mildred rushed to him, crying, "Angelo, Angelo, what is it? What has happened?" Bending over him she gently raised his head and showered unrestrained kisses upon his lips, oblivious of all save her lover.

"Speak! Speak!" she implored.

A faint smile illumined his face; he gazed with ineffable tenderness into her weeping eyes, then slowly closed his own as if in slumber.

THE END